THIS
WILD WEST BOOK
BELONGS TO

LUCKY
JACK

RICO

ALAMEDA SLIM

The WILLIE BROS

DISNEY's

HOME
ON THE
RANGE

SCHOLASTIC INC.

New York   Toronto   London   Auckland   Sydney
Mexico City   New Delhi   Hong Kong   Buenos Aires

"Everybody, this here is Maggie," announced farmer Pearl.

Times were hard for Pearl's little place called Patch of Heaven, but that didn't stop the kindhearted woman from taking in Maggie, a brash cow in need of a home.

The Patch of Heaven animals weren't quite as welcoming as Pearl.

Maggie looked around. The other animals were silently staring at her.

"Now don't everybody speak at one time," Maggie joked.

Prim and proper Mrs. Caloway spoke first. "Good morning, uh, Margaret," she said.

A wide-eyed cow named Grace said, "Hi."

"Wow! You're the biggest cow I've ever seen!" a piglet told Maggie.

Minutes later Sheriff Brown arrived, leaping over a fence on his horse, Buck. "Whoa! Buck, take it easy. This ain't no rodeo!" cried the sheriff. He didn't like excitement, but Buck did.

The sheriff had some bad news for Pearl. "The bank's calling in everybody's debts," Sheriff Brown told Pearl. "If they don't get their money in three days, they're gonna auction off Patch of Heaven!"

"You know, Pearl, it don't have to be this way. All you gotta do is just sell off a few of these critters," he suggested.

But Pearl was furious at the idea. "Stop right there, Sam! They're family. You don't sell family!" she bellowed.

And with that, Pearl chased Sheriff Brown off her farm.

Pearl was heartbroken as she thought about losing her farm. "I'm just plum outta ideas," she told the cows, walking sadly into her house.

Maggie had an idea. "I say we go into town, butter up that sheriff's horse, and get him to give us more time," she declared, picking up the bank notice.

Grace eagerly went along, and Mrs. Caloway eventually followed.

In town, Sheriff Brown received a message that Rico, the bounty hunter, was coming to collect a reward and get his next job.

Buck was excited. His dream was to be a hero. "Boy, wouldn't that be the life?" Buck asked the sheriff's old dog named Rusty. "Riding with Rico! Cleanin' up the West."

When Maggie, Mrs. Caloway, and Grace reached town,
Grace slapped the bank notice onto a barrel in front of Buck.
"Give us three more weeks," Maggie said.
"Your farm is history," Buck interrupted.

Rusty told the cows that they would need $750 to save their farm.
"Where are we going to get that much money?" Grace asked.

Just then Rico galloped into town. He learned that the only outlaw left to catch was Alameda Slim, the cattle rustler.

"What's the bounty?" Rico asked in a low voice.

"Seven hundred and fifty dollars," answered the sheriff.

This gave Maggie an idea:
If the cows caught Alameda Slim,
they could collect the reward and
save Pearl's farm!

"Uh, that's a sensible idea,"
mocked Mrs. Caloway.

"I'm gonna need a fresh horse," Rico told the sheriff.

Buck saw this as his big chance to impress Rico. He raced around, did push-ups, and even tiptoed on the roof!

Rico pointed at Buck. "He'll do." Then Rico saddled him up.

"I'm wearing Rico's saddle!" Buck shouted proudly.

Meanwhile, Maggie and Mrs. Caloway argued about what to do next. The two started fighting, and Grace was caught in the middle!

The dispute caught the sheriff's attention. He thought the three cows belonged to the owner of a wagon, so he tied them to the back of it. Soon the wagon rolled out of town. Buck and Rico headed off in the other direction.

After a while, the wagon and the cows passed a ranch that was being auctioned off.

"What's going to happen to the cow who lived there?" Grace wondered.

"You're looking at her," Maggie answered.

Maggie explained that she used to have a family like the one at Patch of Heaven—until Alameda Slim stole all the cattle and left the rancher penniless.

Night fell as the wagon neared a campsite. Cowboys sat around a blazing fire, while thousands of cattle slept all around them.

Suddenly a gunshot rang out! Before anyone knew what was happening, some cattle rustlers known as the Willie Brothers stormed the campsite. They knocked out all the cowboys and tied them up!

Moments later Alameda Slim thundered in riding his huge buffalo named Junior.

"Come on, girls!" shouted Maggie. "Time to lose these ropes."

Then Maggie charged at Slim. Surprisingly, Slim whipped out his guitar . . .

. . . and started to yodel! Mrs. Caloway and Maggie were spellbound by Slim's yodelling. Only tone-deaf Grace wasn't affected by the sound.

"Maggie, Mrs. Caloway! Snap out of it!" Grace pleaded. Suddenly the wagon started rolling downhill, bumping into Grace and tossing her onto the roof. Next, the wagon scooped up Maggie and Mrs. Caloway. Then Rico and Buck arrived on the scene—only to be sent flying by the out-of-control wagon.

Meanwhile, Slim and the Willies escaped with the herd of cattle.

On their own again, Maggie, Grace, and Mrs. Caloway were more determined than ever to catch Slim and the rustlers. They followed the tracks of the stolen cattle.

"Who better to catch a cattle thief than a cow?" reasoned Grace.

Slim and the Willies had taken the stolen cattle to a deserted mine. Slim was bragging about how he had put most of the local farmers out of business.

Then Slim ducked behind a screen and came back out in different clothes. "This here is the disguise I used to sneak into all them auctions and buy all that land!" he said to the Willies. Then Slim told them how he even used a different name—Y. O'Del.

Slim looked at a map and spotted a farm he hadn't noticed before.
"It's called Patch of Heaven, Uncle Slim," said Phil Willie. "It
goes on auction Thursday morning."

Slim immediately made plans to go to the auction disguised as
Y. O'Del. "Every last acre counts," he sneered, as he branded the
section of the map marked "Patch of Heaven."

Back at Patch of Heaven, things looked grim as the farm and the animals were about to be auctioned.

Pearl worried about her cows. "I don't know what's worse. Losing my farm to the highest bidder or knowin' that my girls are lost out there."

Out in the range, Maggie, Mrs. Caloway, and Grace had met
Lucky Jack, a friendly, peg-legged jackrabbit. They learned that
Lucky Jack had a problem.

"Until recently, I, too, had a home: Echo Mine," he told them
sadly. "Some land grabbin' bandit moved in and flushed us out!"

Jack spotted a wanted poster of Slim and pointed at it. "This is the low-down outlaw who robbed me of my beloved Echo Mine!" he cried.

WANTE

REWA

$750 for the
ALAMED

"You mean this no-good varmint is hiding out in Echo Mine right now?" Maggie asked.

"Without a doubt," responded Jack.

They all agreed to go after Slim together.

27

At the mine, the cows were surprised to see Buck.

"Cows only," Slim's buffalo, Junior, growled.

"We got separated from the herd," Grace told Junior.

So Junior let the cows and Jack enter.

Once inside Slim's hideout, Maggie suggested a plan to the others. "You two get his attention while I sneak up behind him. I'll knock him into the cart. And then we rope him up and wheel him to justice!"

The cows and Jack found Slim counting money. Slim had sold the stolen cattle to Mr. Wesley, a seedy city slicker.

It was time for action! Mrs. Caloway and Grace tossed Slim high into the air. Maggie caught him in a mine cart, and then Lucky Jack quickly tied up Slim. "Let's get outta here!" shouted Grace.

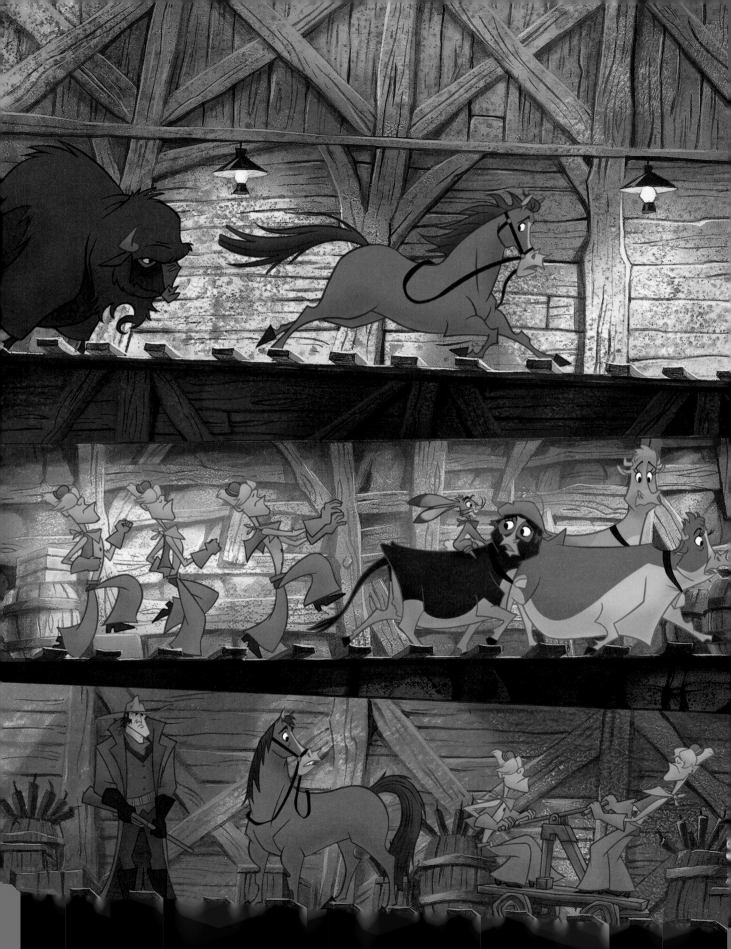

The cows raced to escape with Lucky standing guard over Slim in the cart. The Willies raced to their uncle's rescue. Then Junior, Buck, and even Rico joined the crazy chase through the tunnels.

The whole gang spilled out of the mine, crashing into
Wesley's train full of stolen cattle. Slim broke free of the cart
and captured the cows with a lasso.

When Rico arrived at the scene, Buck overheard Slim
introduce Rico to Wesley. "Let me present the most traitorous,
double-crossin' gun-for-hire that I ever had the pleasure to call
partner," Slim boasted, handing Rico a pile of cash.

"No. It can't be!" Buck whispered to himself. He had
thought Rico was a hero. But Rico was in cahoots with Slim!

Slim put on his disguise and said, "Now if you'll all pardon me, there's a little Patch of Heaven on the auction block this morning."

"He's going to buy our farm," Grace whimpered, as Wesley and the Willies herded the three dairy cows onto the train.

Rico prepared to ride away on Buck. But the horse was furious with Rico.

So Buck decided to give Rico the ride of his life. Buck galloped toward the train, bucking wildly. Maggie, Grace, and Mrs. Caloway watched through the slats of their boxcar.

"Make a break for it, ladies!" Buck called out to them. "Run!"

"Buck, have you gone crazy?" Maggie hollered.

"Maybe I just figured out who the real heroes are!" Buck yelled back.

Maggie, Grace, and Mrs. Caloway smashed against the doors, but the lock wouldn't budge!

"This is useless!" Mrs. Caloway said firmly. "Let's put our heads together! More brains, and less brawn!"

"All right," said Maggie. She took Mrs. Caloway's prized hat off her head and tossed it outside. Enraged, Mrs. Caloway charged the locked door, smashing it to pieces. The cows crashed out of the train.

Buck knocked out the Willie
Brothers with a couple of karate kicks.
Then, together, the three cows
ganged up on Rico.

"Bravo! You stopped Rico cold!" Buck
applauded the cows.

But Pearl's farm was about to be auctioned!
"Unless we sprout wings, we'll never make it back
in time," moaned Grace.

Mrs. Caloway was not about to give up. "This train goes
right by Patch of Heaven!" she exclaimed. "We caught
Slim once, and we shall do it again! Who's with me?"

Quickly Buck freed the cattle from the train.
"Free! We're free!" the cattle shouted joyfully,
as they stampeded onto the prairie.
Then Buck released the cattle cars from the engine.

Maggie, Grace, and Mrs. Caloway started the engine moving. Buck and Lucky Jack jumped on board. They had no time to lose!

The engine raced down the tracks.
Suddenly the group saw another train
heading straight at them!
Just then Jack spotted a
track switch.
"Way ahead of you.
Hop on!" yelled
Buck, and the two
jumped to the ground.

Buck and Jack used Jack's peg leg to flip the switch.
The cows' engine moved safely to another track.
"See ya back at the farm, girls! Good luck!" Buck
called, as the engine sped away.

At Patch of Heaven, the auction was coming to an end. "Sold!" the sheriff proclaimed banging his gavel. Pearl's farm had been bought by Alameda Slim disguised as Y. O'Del.

"O'Del's the name, foreclosure's the game," he snickered to the sheriff.

Pearl watched with a heavy heart. She'd just lost her beloved farm and all her animals!

At that moment the train carrying the cows
sped towards the auction!

"Run for your lives!" yelled the sheriff.

Seconds later Mrs. Caloway, Maggie,
and Grace stood facing Slim. Slim
couldn't believe his eyes.

Grace and Maggie kicked
Slim into the train's smokestack.
Mrs. Caloway blasted
the engine's steam,
and it blew the
disguise off Slim!

"It's Alameda Slim!" the surprised sheriff
shouted. "You're under arrest," the sheriff
declared, as he lassoed the rustler.

Since Pearl's cows had caught Slim, the sheriff gave Pearl
the reward money. "Woo-eee! My farm is saved!" Pearl hooted.
Grace and Mrs. Caloway agreed that the farm was saved
thanks to Maggie's brash ways.

Smiling at her new friends,
Maggie said, "Y'know, maybe
I could hang around awhile."

"How about forever?" Grace suggested.
Maggie couldn't think of anything she would like more!

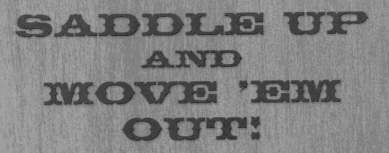

Look back in the story and try to find these pictures